The GREAT EASTER EGG MYSTERY

Written by Fran and Lou Sabin

Illustrated by Irene Trivas

Troll Associates

Library of Congress Cataloging in Publication Data

Sabin, Francene.
    The great Easter egg mystery.

    (A Troll easy-to-read mystery)
    Summary: After working hard to get them painted
in time for the big Easter egg hunt, the Maple
Street Six discover some of their eggs are missing.
    [1. Mystery and detective stories.   2. Easter
stories]   I. Sabin, Louis.   II. Trivas, Irene, ill.
III. Title.   IV. Series: Troll easy-to-read mystery.
PZ7.S1172Gr   [Fic]   81-7610
ISBN 0-89375-604-0 (lib. bdg.)   AACR2
ISBN 0-89375-605-9 (pbk.)

10   9   8   7   6   5   4   3   2

The GREAT EASTER EGG MYSTERY

Eddie Sam

Sue Annie

Sarah Mike

the
Maple Street Six

There were at least a hundred eggs in the Maple Street Six clubhouse. And our job was to paint them, every one of them. That is a lot of eggs for six kids to paint! We did not have much time, either. Just three days until the big Easter-egg hunt!

We all met at the clubhouse after school. Everyone came with a jar of paint. Sue had blue. Eddie had yellow. Sam had red. Annie brought green. Mike had purple. And Sarah—that is me—brought orange. Orange is my favorite color. I am club president. That means I get to choose first.

"All right!" I said. "Let's get to work! Take your brushes and paint!"

"Brushes? I don't have a brush," said Mike.

"Who was going to bring them?" Sue asked.

"Not me," said Annie.

"Not me," said Sam.

"Well, I cannot think of everything!" I told them. "Now we all have to go home and get brushes. Let's go!"

Everybody got back to the clubhouse in a little while, except Sam. "Where is Sam?" Mike asked.

"You know Sam," I said. "He must still be home. Eating."

Just then Sam came in. He had his paintbrush. He also had a peanut-butter-and-jelly sandwich and a banana.

"Okay, we are all here," Annie said. "Listen to this."

Annie is treasurer of the Maple Street Six. That is because she is very good with numbers and plans and things like that.

She held up a chart she made just for egg-painting. On top it said, "Painting Days." On the left side, our names were written. There were numbers all over the rest of the chart. It was really something!

PAINTING DAYS	Day 1	Day 2
Annie	3 hrs	4 hrs.
Eddie	3 "	4 "
Mike	3 "	4 "
Sam	3 "	4 "
Sarah	3	4 "
Sue	3 "	4 "

Annie pointed to her chart. "To start with, there are six of us," she said, "and one hundred eggs. Now, pay attention! We have two days to paint all those eggs. But you have to take away school time, and time for eating and sleeping. That leaves three hours for today, and four hours tomorrow. And—"

"How much time do we get for eating?" Sam cut in. "I need to keep up my energy."

Annie smiled at Sam and kept talking. "Six into a hundred is sixteen, with four eggs left over. And we have seven hours for painting. That means each kid must paint two and two-sevenths eggs every hour."

"What about the four leftover eggs?" asked Eddie. He is good with numbers, too.

Mike fell to the floor, giggling. "We'll give them to Sam," he said. "And he can have my two-sevenths of an egg, too."

I thanked Annie for her treasurer's report. We hung it on the clubhouse wall. Then everybody started to paint.

Sue is our best artist. She put flowers and bunnies and baby chicks on her eggs.

Eddie put stars all over his.

Mike, the club clown, picked up three eggs. "I am Whizzo the Great!" he shouted. He began to juggle the eggs high in the air.

"Stop that right now!" I told Mike. And he stopped—like a statue. But the eggs did not stop. They hit the floor. The shells cracked.

"What a mess!" Eddie moaned.

"I'm glad the eggs are hard-boiled," Sam said. "Or it would really be a mess!"

"Anyway, we can't use those eggs now," I said.

"*I* can," Sam piped up. "I love hard-boiled eggs." And he ate every one.

We all went back to work.

The next day Annie looked unhappy. Her chart showed why. It said: one hundred eggs . . . minus three juggled and eaten . . . minus thirty painted. That left sixty-seven eggs to paint in just one day!

There was no time to talk. No time to fool around. Everybody worked very hard.

Dinner time came, and we still had lots to do. Everybody agreed to come back in an hour with flashlights.

It was spooky. The light from the flashlights made giant shadows on the walls. We heard sounds outside.

"It's the monster!" Mike said. "The one that lives in the woods!"

"*Wooooooo!*" Sue howled.

I knew there was no monster in the woods near our clubhouse. So did all the other kids. But we all jumped. Even Sue.

It was late when we got done with the eggs. And we were tired.

"Let's go home," Sue said.

"No, we can't go yet," Mike said. "We have to put all the eggs back in the box."

"Gee, can't we do that in the morning?" Eddie asked, yawning.

"No, the eggs must be at the town park at nine o'clock," said Annie. "That means we have to be here at eight o'clock —if the eggs *are* in the box. But if the eggs are *not* in the box when we get here, that means we—"

"Okay, Annie! We know!" I said. If I did not stop her, Annie would start another chart.

"I need my sleep," Sue said.

"So do I," Mike said.

Sam jumped up. "I'm not tired!" he said. "You guys go home. I'll put the eggs in the box."

Everybody cheered. And all of us, except Sam, went home.

The Maple Street Six met at the clubhouse at eight o'clock the next morning.

"Wow!" I said. "This place looks great! Sam, you did a super job!"

The paint jars stood in a neat row. The brushes were all stacked together. There was not an egg in sight. There was only the big egg box right in the middle of the table.

"Let me see how the eggs look," Annie said. She lifted the lid of the box. "Oh!" she gasped. "Something is wrong!"

We all looked into the box. Something *was* wrong! There were eleven empty places in the top tray!

"Oh, Sam!" Eddie groaned. "How could you do it?"

Sam's face got red. "Do what?" he asked.

"Darn it, Sam," Mike said. "You only stayed here for the food."

Sam looked hurt. "You think I ate the eggs? Our Easter eggs? I would never do that!"

"He does not belong in our club," Eddie said.

"That is right!" Sue snapped.

"No! The club has rules!" I said. "We have to talk about this, and take a vote. First, we must listen to Sam."

"When I left here last night, all the eggs were in that box," Sam said. He stared hard at the box. "Wait a minute!" he said. "I just remembered—there was someone outside."

"Oh, come on," Annie said. "Who would be out there?"

Sam shook his head. "I was too scared to look."

"I say we should vote him out!" Eddie said.

"Just a minute," I said. "Give Sam a fair chance."

I remembered the sounds we had
heard when we were painting. I
remembered Sue's howl, and our jokes
about a monster. Maybe Sam didn't eat
the eggs. Maybe there was someone
outside. I told everybody what I was
thinking.

"If someone was here," Annie said, "maybe he left a clue."

"Yeah! Let's go!" Mike shouted.

All of us tried to squeeze out the clubhouse door at the same time.

"Look!" Sue pointed to the ground.
There was our first clue. The grass
was pushed down flat. It made a trail
from the clubhouse window to the woods.

Sam was excited. "See? I told you
somebody took our eggs!"

"Maybe," Annie said. "Or maybe *you* took the eggs into the woods, and ate them there."

Mike looked scared. "But maybe there really is a monster! And if we go into the woods, it could eat us all!"

I had to be brave. I was the president!
"Follow me!" I told them. "We will solve
this mystery!"

We followed the trail to the edge of
the woods.

"Come here!" Sam cried out.

We rushed over to him. At his feet was
a piece of eggshell. It was light blue.

"Now that *is* a clue!" I said.

Eddie picked up the eggshell. "No, it is not," he said glumly. "It's from a robin's egg."

We all looked up. There was a nest in a tree high above us.

I sighed. "Oh, well. Let's keep hunting."

We went into the woods. It was cool and quiet, except for the bubbling of water in the stream.

"I have an idea," Annie said. "If we all walk together, we can search just one place. But if we spread out, we can search six places."

That made sense. We went different ways. "Call out if you find a clue," I said.

"*AHHHHHHHHHHHH!*" Sue shrieked. She was at the edge of the stream. "Come quickly! Somebody has been killed! The water is full of blood!"

We ran to the stream. There *was* blood in the water!

"I'm not staying here anymore!" Eddie said in a shaky voice. "We better get the police!"

Suddenly, Mike laughed. "We are silly."

"What's silly about a murder?" Eddie asked.

"What murder?" Mike said. "No one was killed. Unless it was someone who bleeds yellow . . . and green . . . and purple . . ."

We stared into the stream. Mike was right. The water was a lot of colors now.

"I bet it's paint," Sam said. "Someone is throwing our Easter eggs into the stream! Come on! Maybe we can catch the thief!"

We walked along the stream. We were as quiet as could be.

Suddenly, we heard sounds! Splashing sounds! We looked through the trees.

"Oh, aren't they cute," Annie whispered.

"There are your horrible monsters," Sam said.

At the edge of the stream was a family of raccoons—a mother and three babies. And there were some of our Easter eggs! The mother raccoon was washing them in the water. Then she was feeding them to her babies.

"Let's not bother them," I said.

"Yes," Mike said. "We don't need so many eggs for the party."

"The party!" Annie said. "It's almost time for the Easter-egg hunt!"

We ran back to the clubhouse and got the eggs. We took them to the park. Then we hid them before all the neighborhood kids got there. We had to work fast.

The Maple Street Six finished just in time. We sat on top of a hill and watched the Easter-egg hunt. Everybody had a great time!

"Boy, am I hungry!" Sam said.

We all laughed. "Let's take a vote," I said. "Who thinks Sam is the best member of the club?"

"We do!" everybody sang out.

Sam looked happy. He was even
happier when we voted to buy him a big
ice-cream soda. And we ran down the hill
all the way to the soda shop!